JINX GLOVE

JINX GLOVE

by
MATT CHRISTOPHER

Illustrated by Norm Chartier

Little, Brown and Company
BOSTON   TORONTO

FIRST EDITION

T 06/74

Library of Congress Cataloging in Publication Data

Christopher, Matthew F
  Jinx glove.

  [1. Baseball--Stories] I. Title.
PZ7.C458Ji   [Fic]
ISBN 0-316-13965-3   73-12836

Published simultaneously in Canada
by Little, Brown & Company (Canada) Limited

PRINTED IN THE UNITED STATES OF AMERICA

to Chris, Ricky and Michael

Chip pounded his fist hard into the worn pocket of the old glove. How he longed for a brand-new one! He had hoped he would have it for this game that his team, the Red Barons, was playing against the Hawks. But his father had used the old glove when he had played. Would he let Chip get a new one?

Crack! A smashing grounder to Chip at third base! He caught the ball just behind the bag and pegged it to first. Out!

"Nice play, Chip!" pitcher Fred Bonner yelled.

The next Hawk up lined a sharp drive over short, then scored on a long triple. Chip's heart sank. Now that the Hawks had scored first, the Red Barons had to play much harder.

Suddenly a waist-high line drive streaked toward Chip. The ball went right into the pocket of his glove, and he touched third base before the surprised runner could tag up.

A double play! Three outs!

The Red Barons batted, but couldn't get a man on. The Hawks scored twice in the top of the fourth inning to go into the lead, 3–0.

In the bottom of the fourth Mick Rundle hit a double to left field, Jason Hill flied out, and Chip came to bat. His heart pounded as he watched the Hawks' pitcher, Ned Kish, deliver the pitch.

Bang! Like a shot the ball sailed out to left field for a hit! Mick Rundle scored. Then Chip scored on Mark Andrews' single. That was it for the inning. Hawks 3, Red Barons 2.

The game ended with that score. The Red Barons went home, disappointed that they lost, but happy that they weren't beaten more badly. The Hawks were the toughest team in the league.

At the supper table Chip thought again of a new glove. "Dad, may I get a new glove?" he asked. "Mine is so old it's ready to fall apart."

His father shrugged. "It looks fine to me, but okay. You'll have to use your own money, you know."

Chip sighed. He had a paper route and had saved up nearly twenty dollars. He had hoped, though, that his father would give him the money.

"Okay," Chip said, then looked his father squarely in the eyes. He knew how much his father had liked that old glove. "Dad, would you mind if—if I threw the old one away?"

His father frowned but said, "Of course not, Chip. It's yours to do with as you wish."

The next morning Chip headed for the heart of Mulberry City, his wallet in his pocket, his old glove in his hand. He came alongside Mulberry Lake and threw the glove as far over it as he could. It made a big splash and disappeared.

For a moment Chip squeezed his eyes shut and held his breath. Then he relaxed.

He turned to go on and saw a small, barefooted kid looking at him. The kid looked familiar, although Chip was sure he had never seen him before.

"Why did you do that?" the boy said.

"Do you think you'd want that glove?" asked Chip.

The kid shrugged.

"You wouldn't," Chip said. "It was ready to fall apart."

Chip turned and left the lake. He
went downtown and bought a brand-
new glove at a sporting goods store. He
held it on his hand all the way home. It
was neat. Bright yellow, with a soft
pocket.

The Red Barons' next game was on
Thursday, against the Pirates. Chip
stood at third, his brand-new glove
shining like a chunk of gold. He couldn't
wait for the ball to be hit to him.

"Let 'im hit it, Fred!" he yelled.

Crack! A sizzling grounder came
directly at Chip! The ball struck the
heel of his glove and bounced off! By
the time he picked it up, the runner
was safe.

"Butterfingers!" Mick Rundle yelled.
The Pirates picked up two runs that
inning. In the third Chip fumbled the ball
twice. He couldn't believe it! Was there
something wrong with his new glove?

"Throw that mitt away and get back your old one!" Mick shouted to him.

The Red Barons lost the game, 8—3.

"I just had a bad day," Chip said as he walked home with Mick and some of the other guys.

"Oh, sure," Mick grunted.

When they reached the corner of the block, Chip and all the guys except Mick turned left. Mick lived somewhere by the lake.

"He's sure touchy," Chip said after Mick had left. "Every time I made an error he yelled at me."

"He yells at me, too," center fielder Jason Hill said. "Don't let him bug you."

No matter what Jason said, though,
it wasn't easy for Chip to forget Mick's
yelling. He just *had* to play lots better
baseball in the next game.

He didn't.

Two days later, in the very first
inning against the Falcons, he dropped
an easy fly. In the second inning he
missed a grounder. Before the inning
was over four runs had scored.

Chip felt lucky that his batting was lots better than his fielding. He drilled a double between left and center fields and smashed out a home run that tied up the score. Then Mick socked a homer that won the ball game, 7–6.

"My new glove is a jinx," Chip said at the supper table. "I just can't catch beans with it."

26

His sister, Marge, laughed. "You're
not supposed to catch beans," she said.
"You're supposed to catch baseballs."

"Very funny," Chip said. "Ha-ha."

"What did you do with the old one?"
his father asked.

"I threw it into the lake," Chip
answered sadly. He paused, and then
his eyes brightened. "Know what? I'm
going to try to find it!"

The next morning he went to the lake with his swim trunks under his clothes. Once there he removed his clothes and swam out to where he had thrown the glove.

He swam around near the bottom
until he was out of breath. He rose to
the surface, filled his lungs with air,
and swam down deep again.

He couldn't find his glove, so he gave up.

He waited on shore for his trunks to
dry before he put on his pants.

"Hi," he heard someone say. He
looked around and saw the kid he had
seen the other day.

"Hi," Chip greeted him. Then Chip's
eyes almost bugged out of his head.
The kid was holding his old glove!

31

"Where'd you get *that*?" Chip cried.

"Mick got it for me," the kid answered. "I told him I saw you throw the glove in the lake and he swam out and got it."

"It's mine," Chip said, reaching for it. "Will you give it back to me, please?"

"Nope. It's mine, now," the kid said. He turned and ran between two houses and out of sight.

Chip shook his head sadly. Well, the kid was right, in a way. The glove *was* his, now.

Chip didn't wait any longer to let his trunks dry. He put on his clothes and left.

"I'll never get my old glove back,"
he told Marge. "A kid's got it, and he
won't give it to me."

The day came when the Red Barons played the Hawks again. It was the Big Game, because if the Hawks beat the Red Barons once more, the Red Barons could not end the season in the top three.

Chip caught the first two grounders
hit to him during the first and second
innings. But he missed one in the third
that helped the Hawks score two runs.

"Butterfingers!" Mick yelled at him.
Chip blushed.

By the bottom of the fifth inning the Hawks were leading, 5–3.

Chip felt so awful that he could have gone home right then.

When his turn came to bat, though, he knocked a single, then scored on Mark's triple. Buck Neeley walked. Then Sam Polowski hit a double to score him. Hawks 5, Red Barons 5.

Chip started out to third, then changed his mind. Why should he go out there and keep making errors? For the team's sake someone should take his place.

"Coach Haley," he said, "I don't
think I . . ."

"Chip!" a thin voice shouted.

Chip turned and saw the kid who
had his old glove running toward him.
"Here!" the kid cried, and held out the
glove.

Chip's heart drummed. "You, you mean it?" he asked.

"Yes," said the kid. "It looks like you really need it."

"Thanks, kid!" Chip said.

"What were you going to say to me, Chip?" the coach asked.

"Nothing," said Chip, smiling.

Wearing his old glove he caught two grounders in a row. With two men on and two outs, the Hawks seemed sure to score. Then Chip caught a high pop fly that ended the inning.

The Red Barons came to bat, scored, and won the game, 6–5.

Chip, as happy as a pup at mealtime, looked for the kid who had returned his glove, and saw him walking off the field with Mick.

"Kid! Mick!" Chip yelled, and ran after them. "Mick, this kid told me you dove into the lake for this old glove."

"I did," Mick said. "He's my brother Pete, you know. Our folks said they couldn't afford a new glove for him, and you sure didn't want yours. So I dove in and got it for him."

"Wait here, Pete," Chip said. He ran to the dugout, got his new glove, and ran back with it.

"Here, Pete," he said. "It's yours."

Pete's eyes widened. "You sure it's okay?" he asked.

"Yes, I'm sure," Chip said. "*Real sure!*" And he ran all the way home with his old glove to show it to his family.

Especially to his father, who had used it before he had.

47

Books by Matt Christopher

Sports Stories

THE LUCKY BASEBALL BAT
BASEBALL PALS
BASKETBALL SPARKPLUG
TWO STRIKES ON JOHNNY
LITTLE LEFTY
TOUCHDOWN FOR TOMMY
LONG STRETCH AT FIRST BASE
BREAK FOR THE BASKET
TALL MAN IN THE PIVOT
CHALLENGE AT SECOND BASE
CRACKERJACK HALFBACK
BASEBALL FLYHAWK
SINK IT, RUSTY
CATCHER WITH A GLASS ARM
WINGMAN ON ICE
TOO HOT TO HANDLE
THE COUNTERFEIT TACKLE
THE RELUCTANT PITCHER
LONG SHOT FOR PAUL
MIRACLE AT THE PLATE
THE TEAM THAT COULDN'T LOSE
THE YEAR MOM WON THE PENNANT
THE BASKET COUNTS
HARD DRIVE TO SHORT
CATCH THAT PASS!
SHORTSTOP FROM TOKYO
LUCKY SEVEN
JOHNNY LONG LEGS
LOOK WHO'S PLAYING FIRST BASE
TOUGH TO TACKLE
THE KID WHO ONLY HIT HOMERS
FACE-OFF
MYSTERY COACH
ICE MAGIC
NO ARM IN LEFT FIELD
JINX GLOVE
FRONT COURT HEX

Animal Stories

DESPERATE SEARCH
STRANDED

E
C

11819

Christopher, Matt

Jinx Glove

DATE	ISSUED TO
	Jonathan 2
	FEB. 22 2002